Wang Yuwei

# Mr. Cat
## and the Little Girl

Clavis

**NEW YORK**

Winter has come early this year.
Thousands of snowflakes are **WHIRLING** down.

*What a picture*, thinks Mr. Cat as he looks outside.
*I would love to capture it.*
He grabs his painting materials and walks outside.
Step, step, step, with his paws through the snow.

There are still many autumn leaves on the ground.
Mr. Cat sees red leaves, yellow leaves, brown leaves . . .
and he sees a green leaf.

Mr. Cat lifts it up in astonishment.
He can't believe what he sees.
There's a girl under the leaf!
**SHE'S SMALL**. VERY SMALL.

Mr. Cat picks her up. The sleeping girl feels cold,
but she quickly warms up in his fluffy paws.

Mr. Cat can't leave
her here in the cold snow.
He decides to take her home.

The next morning, Mr. Cat
wakes from a soft tickle on his ear.
He opens one eye and then the other.
On his pillow he sees the little girl giggling softly.


Mr. Cat makes breakfast for himself and for the girl.
Fish for himself and toast for her.

Mr. Cat has never made toast before and he burns it a bit,
but the little girl doesn't mind.

"Get off my **TAIL!**"

"Don't touch the **PAINT!**"

Mr. Cat isn't used to having a little girl in his studio.
He can't paint like this!
But the girl is happy. She laughs and she dances and . . .

**BANG!**
**BOOM!**
**FLASH!**

She tips a vase
over and it falls
on her foot.
She starts to cry.

Mr. Cat is no longer angry.
"It's okay, little one," he says gently.
"Shall I make a nice drawing for you?"

The girl dries her tears
and she nods yes.

They take a walk together through the snow.

Mr. Cat is surprised. He notices that yellow flowers appear
in the middle of the snow,
right on the spots where the little girl walks.

### IT'S BEAUTIFUL!
Mr. Cat makes a sketch of the flowers,
so he can paint them at home
in the most vibrant shades of yellow.

When they get home he finds that the plant
that fell on the girl's foot has started to grow.

# BIGGER ...
## AND BIGGER ...
## AND BIGGER ...

Until the plant almost fills the entire room!

Mr. Cat is worried.
What if the plant continues to grow?
There won't be enough space for him and the girl!

Maybe it's a magical plant?
Mr. Cat starts searching for it
in an encyclopedia.
But instead of the plant,
he finds a picture of the girl.
With a text next to it:

Born in the first snow.
Can affect the growth of plants.
Lifetime . . . one winter.

Mr. Cat shuts the book with a smack.
He stares at the girl in silence.
He feels sad . . .

## ...BUT ALSO FULL OF INSPIRATION!

Mr. Cat can't stop painting.
He makes one portrait of the girl after another.
And the girl joins him.
She makes drawings of Mr. Cat.

They take a break and eat delicious doughnuts.
And when it gets very late, Mr. Cat and the girl
crawl into the warm bed.
Then Mr. Cat reads her a bedtime story.
"Once upon a time there was a very, very little girl . . ."

The next day Mr. Cat and
the girl go for a walk again.

More and more flowers appear
under the girl's feet.

Even the plant indoors gets flowers.

**MMM, THEY SMELL
DELICIOUS...**

The girl begins to sleep more often.

Mr. Cat doesn't want to sleep.
He stays awake watching the girl,
even though he's very tired.

Winter is almost over.
It will be spring soon.

Mr. Cat made breakfast.
He's waiting for the girl.

But she doesn't show up.

Mr. Cat is

# WORRIED.

He looks and looks for the girl,
but he can't find her anywhere.

Mr. Cat feels a tickle on his tail.
Maybe the girl is sleeping there?
But he doesn't dare to look.
He's too afraid that she's already gone.

It's quiet in his house.
And lonely.

Mr. Cat sighs.
He spends his time painting and taking care of the plant.

The seasons pass.
The world is white again.

A few autumn leaves are still on the ground.

Mr. Cat is filled with new hope.
Maybe, he thinks, the girl will be there again,
under a green leaf
in the forest . . .